This
MOUSE ✺ WORKS
Classics Collection Storybook

belongs to

_____

DISNEP's

THE JUNGLE BOOK

CLASSIC STORYBOOK

MOUSE WORKS

© 1986, 1995 Disney Enterprises, Inc.

Printed in the United States of America

ISBN: 1-57082-239-X

7 9 10 8

One day, deep in the jungle, a panther named Bagheera discovered a baby tucked inside a shipwrecked boat.

Bagheera left the child outside the den of a new wolf family, hoping they would care for it. To his relief, after a few curious sniffs, the mother wolf took the baby inside her cave.

For ten years, the boy — who came to be known as Mowgli — was raised as a wolf cub. He loved his animal family, and he was a favorite with all the members of the wolf pack. Bagheera often visited him, and was pleased to see how happy Mowgli was in his adopted home. Yet, Bagheera knew that someday Mowgli would have to return to his own kind.

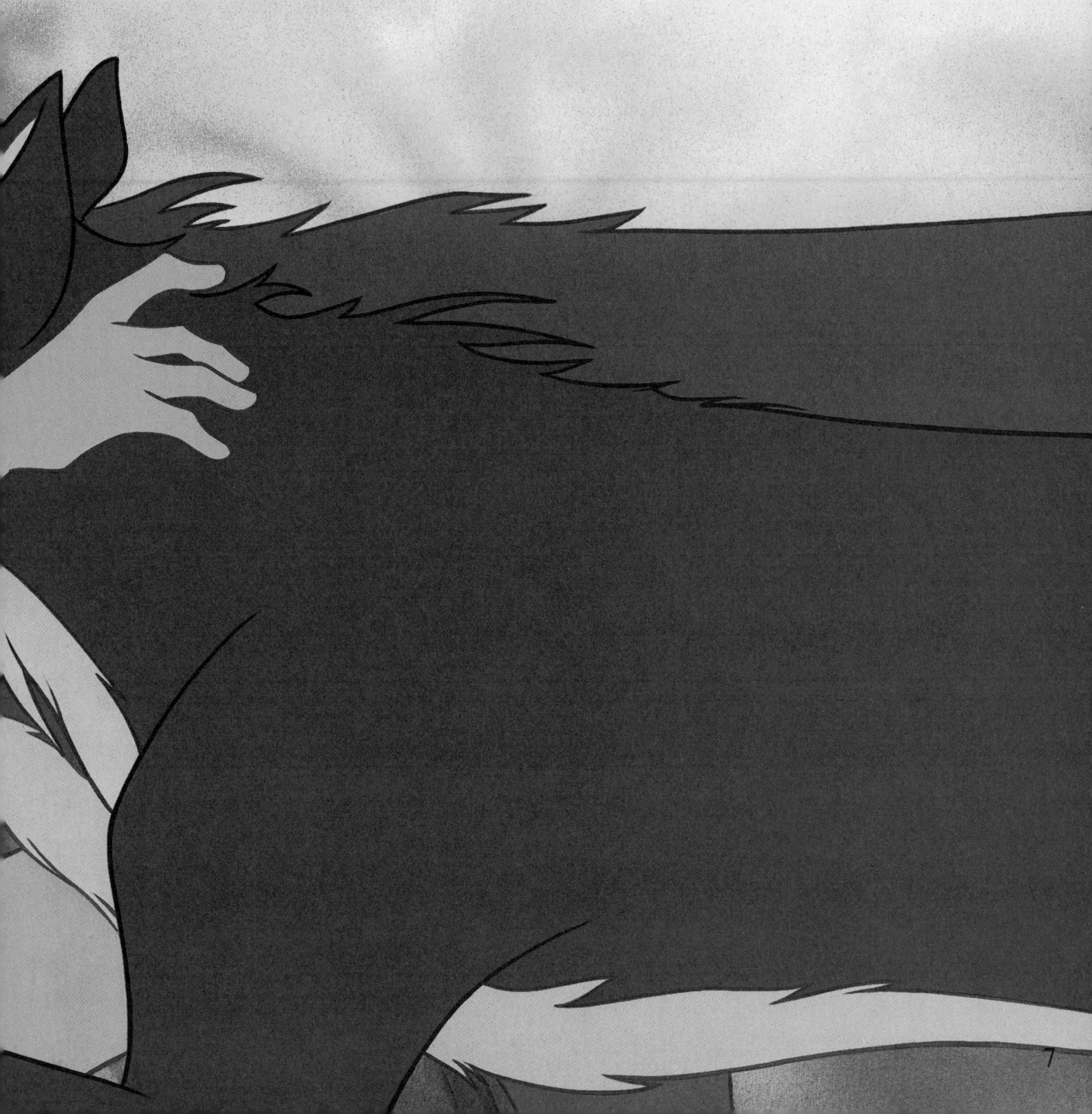

One night, the wolf elders called a meeting at
Council Rock. Akela, their leader, told them that the
fierce tiger Shere Khan had returned to their part of
the jungle. Fearing that Mowgli would grow up to be
a hunter, Shere Khan intended to destroy the boy. The
elders soon decided that Mowgli would have to leave,
for his own safety as well as the pack's.

Akela told Rama, Mowgli's father, the bad news.

"But the boy cannot survive alone in the jungle," Rama protested.

"Perhaps I can be of help," offered Bagheera. "I know of a Man-village where he will be safe."

"Then so be it," said Akela. "Go quickly, for there is no time to lose."

So Bagheera and Mowgli took off through the jungle.

"I'm taking you to a Man-village," Bagheera told
Mowgli. And then he explained about Shere Khan.
"I can look after myself!" Mowgli insisted.

"We'll spend the night here," Bagheera said as they settled on the branch of a tall tree.

But just as Bagheera was drifting off to sleep, Kaa the snake appeared. "What a delicious Man-cub!" he hissed.

Mowgli just wanted to be left alone. "Oh, go away!" he told Kaa grumpily. Instead, the snake used the special power of his hypnotic eyes to put Mowgli in a trance.

As Mowgli fell into a trance, Kaa wrapped his coils around the boy's body.

Suddenly Bagheera realized what was happening, and jumped up and hit Kaa — SMACK! — on top of the head.

The snake angrily slithered away with a knot in his tail!

The next morning, Bagheera and Mowgli awoke to
a rumbling and shaking beneath them.

"A parade!" shouted Mowgli excitedly as he
grabbed a vine and swung down to get a better look.

Bagheera just covered his ears. "Oh, no. The dawn
patrol again," he said wearily.

Within seconds, a column of singing elephants led by Colonel Hathi marched into view. The Colonel ran his herd like an army, and he demanded order and discipline from everyone in it — including his baby boy.

Mowgli thought the elephant parade was grand. "Hello!" he said as he ran up to the baby elephant. "Can I do what you're doing, too?"

"Sure," the little elephant told him. "But don't talk in the ranks. It's against regulations!"

Mowgli dropped down to the ground and began to march on all fours. But when Colonel Hathi ordered his troops to turn the other way, Mowgli kept right on going forward. BONK! He bumped straight into his new friend!

Next it was time for inspection. All the elephants stood at attention while Colonel Hathi checked their trunks one by one. When it was Mowgli's turn, the boy stuck out his nose as far as he could.

"What happened to your trunk?" demanded the
Colonel as he picked Mowgli up for a closer look.
"Why — you're a Man-cub!" he sputtered.

Just then Bagheera appeared. "The Man-cub is with me," he said, "and I'm taking him back to the Man-village to stay. You have my word."

"Good, because remember, an elephant never forgets," Colonel Hathi replied.

Bagheera insisted on taking Mowgli to the Man-village that very moment. But the Man-cub refused to go.

"Then from now on, you're on your own!" Bagheera told him. And then he watched as Mowgli walked off into the jungle.

When Mowgli stopped to rest, a big, carefree bear named Baloo wandered by. Baloo could see that Mowgli had a few lessons to learn if he was to survive in the jungle.

Baloo taught Mowgli how to get tasty food like ants and bananas and coconuts without working too hard.

The two new friends jumped into the water and floated lazily down the river. "You're gonna make one swell bear," said Baloo. Mowgli had to agree that Baloo's life sure was a lot of fun.

Suddenly, Mowgli's peaceful bear ride came to
an end when a monkey leaned down and snatched
him right off of Baloo's stomach.

"Hey! Let go of me!" Mowgli cried as the
mischievous monkeys tossed him around.

11

"Give me back my Man-cub!" demanded Baloo as he shook his fist at the pranksters. But some of the monkeys were already carrying Mowgli off into the jungle.

Soon Mowgli found himself face-to-face with King Louie, an orangutan who desperately wanted to be a man. The king hoped Mowgli could teach him how to make fire.

45

Up on a balcony in King Louie's temple, Baloo and Bagheera heard everything.

"You create a disturbance," Bagheera instructed Baloo, "and I'll rescue Mowgli."

Thinking quickly, Baloo disguised himself as an ape and burst through the door, dancing and singing. King Louie grabbed him by the hand, and together they moved across the courtyard, swinging each other this way and that.

Meanwhile, Bagheera kept trying to rescue Mowgli. But every time he got close, Mowgli danced out of reach.

Then something terrible happened. Baloo's
costume fell off right in front of King Louie!
"It's Baloo the bear!" shouted the monkeys.

52

In the rumpus that broke out, King Louie's
temple began to fall down. Baloo tricked the
orangutan into holding up part of it — but then,
Baloo got stuck holding up a section himself.

Rocks from the collapsing temple showered down around them, when Baloo finally let go of the temple roof. The three took off into the jungle making their escape.

"Man, that's what I call a swingin' party!" exclaimed Baloo.

That night, Bagheera convinced
Baloo that living in the jungle put
Mowgli in danger. When Baloo
told Mowgli that it was time to go
to the Man-village, the Man-cub
ran off into the bush.

Not far away, Shere Khan prowled through the tall grass, waiting for some unsuspecting prey.

Shere Khan's hunting ended before it began, however, when Colonel Hathi's brigade came stomping through the bush. Bagheera heard the elephants, too, and went to ask for the Colonel's help in finding Mowgli.

No one knew it, but at that very moment
Mowgli was in the clutches of Kaa the snake.

But the snake was interrupted by a yanking on his tail. "I'd like a word with you, if you don't mind," Shere Khan called to Kaa.

"What a surprise!" the snake replied nervously. He didn't want Shere Khan to know he had Mowgli up in the tree. He wanted that Man-cub for himself!

"I thought perhaps you were entertaining someone up there," said the tiger menacingly.

"Oh, no!" protested Kaa.

"Then I'm sure you wouldn't mind showing me your coils," Shere Khan replied. What could Kaa do? He slithered out of the tree, freeing Mowgli as he went.

After Shere Khan had gone, Mowgli slid down a vine and ran to safety. He had learned better than to trust that tricky snake Kaa!

Later that afternoon, Mowgli came upon four very bored and silly vultures. The birds began teasing him, but Mowgli looked so lonely and sad that the group decided to make friends with him instead.

Mowgli's new vulture friends didn't stand by him for very long, however. The minute they caught sight of Shere Khan, the birds abandoned Mowgli and flew to safety.

Shere Khan was amused by Mowgli's courage and gave him a chance at a head start. But Mowgli just stood in front of him, refusing to move. The tiger lost his patience and tried to lunge at the boy with his razor-sharp claws.

Luckily for Mowgli, Baloo had the tiger by the tail.

"Run, Mowgli, run!" the bear shouted as he held on tight. The vultures picked up Mowgli and flew him out of Shere Khan's reach.

80

Suddenly, the sky darkened, and lightning
struck a nearby tree. That's when the birds told
Mowgli a secret: fire was the one thing Shere
Khan feared.

"Let me go!" cried Mowgli. "Baloo needs help!" He grabbed a burning tree limb while the vultures dive-bombed Shere Khan's head.

While Shere Khan tried to fight off the vultures, Mowgli crept up behind him and tied the burning stick to his tail. The terrified tiger ran into the jungle as fast as he could.

When the vultures went to congratulate
Mowgli, they found him kneeling beside his
dear friend Baloo.

"Baloo, get up. Oh, please get up," Mowgli begged. The courageous bear lay perfectly still as the cool rain fell all around them.

After a long while Baloo opened his eyes,
pretending he'd been fine right along.

"I never felt better. I was just takin' five.
Playin' it cool," he explained.

Mowgli just had to laugh and give him a
big bear hug.

By this time, Bagheera had arrived, and the three friends set off through the jungle once more. As they neared the Man-village, Mowgli spotted a pretty young girl collecting water by the river.

"Look, what's that?" he asked his pals.

"Forget about those. They ain't nothing but trouble," Baloo told him.

But Mowgli was curious and crept off to take a closer look. "I've never seen one before!" he exclaimed.

Baloo and Bagheera watched as Mowgli picked up the girl's water jug and followed her. As Mowgli walked through the entrance of the village, he turned to smile at his old friends.

"It was bound to happen, Baloo," Bagheera
said. "Mowgli is where he belongs now."
Then he and Bagheera sang a little song as
they strolled back into the jungle arm-in-arm.

For you... from MOUSE WORKS

A special invitation to have even more fun— Free!

Send for a FREE ISSUE of FamilyFun Magazine! It's chock full of fun activities the whole family will love!

⭐ Easy after-school and rainy-day activities. Like how to create a cloud – or make tin-can stilts!

⭐ Great crafts & hobbies with step-by-step instructions. Like how to splatter a T-shirt or make thrilling, chilling Halloween costumes!

⭐ Fun party plans, dynamite decorations, and great games. Like how to dance the hula in a paper grass skirt and make a lei out of pasta!

⭐ Recipes kids love to make – and eat! Imagine carrot "coins", broccoli "trees", and baked potatoes "a la Mode."

⭐ And everything else fun from family computing to family traveling to Family Olympics. Imagine tie-dying socks – or making "duck feet" to have a Duck Foot Relay Race!

SPECIAL JOKES & GAMES FOR KIDS

FamilyFun
Halloween Party!
Slimy Games, Zany Food & Other Wicked Fun
Make-your-own Costumes

"What's for Dinner?"
12 Award-winners Kids Eat Up

Teaching Kids About Money
An Age-by-age Activity Guide

Dude Ranch Roundup

The Joy of Autumn
Leaf Games, and a Friend...

You always know what you'll find in FamilyFun – 100% activities and 100% fun! And it's free with this special invitation!

Just send in the FREE ISSUE Certificate today!

FamilyFun
Free Issue Certificate

Yes! Send my family the next issue of FamilyFun – FREE! If we like it, we'll get a full year (10 big issues in all, including my free issue and TWO SPECIAL ISSUES) for just $11.95. We'll SAVE 54% off the cover price! If we choose not to subscribe, we'll return the bill marked "cancel", and owe nothing. The FREE issue is ours to keep.

Name _____ (please print)

Address _____

City/State/Zip _____

(Optional) gender of child/children (boy/girl) _____ Birthdate(s) _____

FamilyFun's newsstand price is $25.90 a year. In Canada, add $10 (U.S. funds) for postage and GST. Other foreign orders, add $20 (U.S. funds). First issue mails within 6-8 weeks. Offer valid through June 30, 2000. © Disney

FamilyFun HOLIDAYS SPECIAL ISSUE
Best Toys 3rd Annual T.O.Y. Awards 46-Page Guide
Kids' Crafts Cards, Gifts & Ornaments
Parties & Games

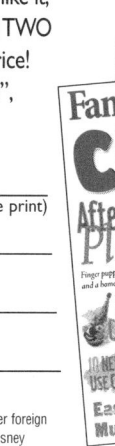

FamilyFun Special Issue
CRAFTS
After-School Play!
Finger puppets, model boats, and a homemade birdhouse
26 WACKY CUPCAKES
10 NEW ways to USE CRAYONS
Easy Musical...

Includes **TWO SPECIAL ISSUES** at no extra cost!

L7MW

FamilyFun

100% activities. 100% fun.

From Disney

"Your magazine is absolutely fantastic! It has everything I have been looking for in a magazine and have never been able to find."
— Peggy Bertsch, Sandusky, Ohio

"Fresh ideas for getting involved with my kids — isn't that what parenting is all about? Thank you, thank you, thank you."
— Cathy Zirkelbach, Denver, Colorado

"This is the best magazine for families I have ever seen. I will keep my issues forever."
— Carol A. Green, Lee's Summit, Missouri

"I have read FamilyFun front to back twice and have shared articles with almost everyone I know. Our family has tried recipes and activities — and we haven't had a flop yet! I only wish we had discovered you sooner."
— Mary Balcom, Rochester Hills, Michigan

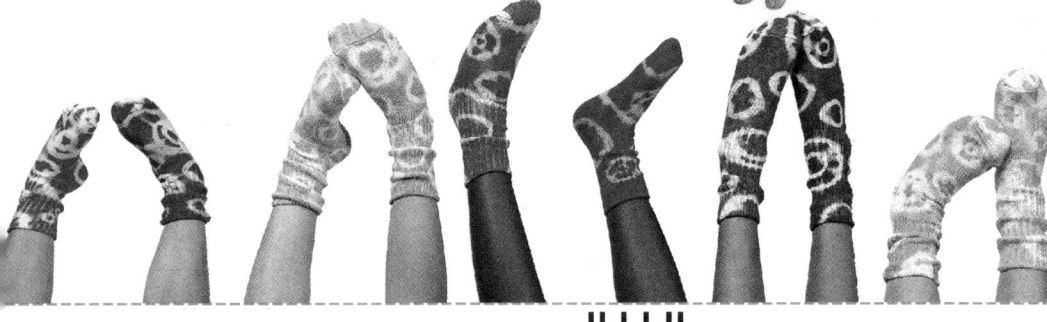

FREE ISSUE!

Yours free!
See why families everywhere are having so much fun with FamilyFun! Send for your FREE ISSUE today. If card is missing, write to FamilyFun Magazine, PO Box 37031, Boone, IA 50037-2031.